GIANT TROUBLE

HAMSTER PRINCESS
GIANT TROUBLE

BY

Ursula Vernon

Dial Books for Young Readers

Dial Books for Young Readers
Penguin Young Readers Group
An imprint of Penguin Random House LLC
375 Hudson Street
New York, New York 10014

Copyright © 2017 by Ursula Vernon

ISBN 9780399186523
Printed in China

10   9   8   7   6   5   4   3   2   1

Design by Jennifer Kelly
Text set in Minister Std Light

For Mz. Faunce

CHAPTER 1

Harriet Hamsterbone was dripping wet and shivering with cold, and she had never been happier.

She had spent the last two hours climbing up a hundred-foot cliff and throwing herself off the top into the river. It had been a good day.

"Cliff-diving," she said to her faithful battle quail, Mumfrey. "Do you know how much I've missed cliff-diving?"

"Qwerk," said Mumfrey, which is Quail for "I may have some idea, yes."

Harriet was a princess, heir to the throne of the hamster king, and she had not been cliff-diving in ages. She had been very fond of it when she was young and (owing to a fairy curse) invincible, but once the curse wore off, she'd had to give it up. Cliff-diving is not a terribly safe sport. Her mother had never approved.

Another fairy had recently given Harriet back her ability to cliff-dive, as thanks for breaking the curse on twelve dancing mouse princesses, and Harriet intended to make the most of it.

"I would have saved them anyway," she told Mumfrey. "I mean, they needed help, and clearly nobody else was going to do it. But the cliff-diving is a nice bonus." She shook the water out of her ears.

"Qwerk," agreed Mumfrey.

"It's definitely magic too! I could feel it!" (There are approximately six thousand ways that one can cliff-dive wrong, almost all of which are fatal. Harriet had slipped on one of the jumps and the magic had actually swooped in, pointed her toes correctly, and gotten her lined up with the water in the proper fashion. This was why Harriet was not spread across the landscape as hamster jam. Did we mention that cliff-diving was a *very* dangerous sport?)

"Qwerk . . ."

"Still, I suppose we should be getting back home."

"Qwerk!"

She was fluffing up her damp fur and feeling generally good about life, when a cloaked figure stepped out from behind the bushes.

One of the downsides to being a famous warrior princess is that cloaked figures are always jumping out at you from behind bushes. There were days when Harriet had no fewer than three people in cloaks to deal with. She was good at it, but it did get tiresome.

She snatched up her sword from where it hung on Mumfrey's saddle and pointed it at the figure. "Halt! Are you an assassin?"

"Um," said the figure, looking at the sword. "No."

"Evil wizard?"

Harriet sighed.

She would almost have rather dealt with an assassin. People throwing poisoned daggers at you was annoying, but you didn't feel rude whacking them with your sword afterward. People trying to sell you things made it terribly awkward to refuse.

"Right," she said wearily. "Get it over with."

The figure coughed. "Where was I?"

YOU JUST SAID "PRINCESS!" VERY DRAMATICALLY.

"Right. Yes. Thank you. Princess!" cried the cloaked figure. "I have an offer for you that only a fool would refuse!"

"How did you know I was a princess?"

The cloaked figure had a striped face and appeared to be a chipmunk. "I don't," he admitted. "But you're wearing a tiara, so you're either a princess or you *think* you're a princess, and I'm trying to sell you something here, so I'm happy to go along with your delusions."

"Fair enough," said Harriet. She admired honesty in salespeople. "What're you selling?"

The chipmunk reached into his cape pocket and presented his goods with a flourish.

BEHOLD!

". . . those are beans," said Harriet.

"Yes!" said the chipmunk. "The finest beans in all the land! And I will trade three of them to you for the quail you are riding."

"No deal," said Harriet. "Mumfrey is my best friend. He isn't for sale. And also, those're *beans*."

"Perhaps you do not quite understand, Princess," said the chipmunk. "For these are no ordinary beans. They're *magic!*"

Harriet stifled another sigh. The world was full of magic, and she had encountered quite a lot of it, although she herself was about as magical as a rock. (Except for the cliff-diving thing.)

Unfortunately, the world was also full of people trying to sell you something by claiming it was magical. Harriet's dad had a real problem with this, and had acquired an entire room full of gadgets that were supposed to slice vegetables at a touch, remove blemishes, and reduce eye wrinkles, all sold to him by smooth-talking salesmen. None of them worked at all, although the one that reduced eye wrinkles would explode if you pulled the wrong lever.

"I don't care if they wear little tutus and do a dance," said Harriet. "I wouldn't trade Mumfrey for three magic beans."

"Qwerk," said Mumfrey, satisfied.

"Are you sure?" asked the chipmunk, waving his handful under Harriet's nose. "Because these are some *seriously* magical beans."

"Not interested," said Harriet.

"You don't find beans like this every day."

"Really, *truly* not interested," said Harriet.

"In fact, these are quite possibly the most magical beans that have ever—HEY!"

"Mumfrey!"

The chipmunk had waved his hand too close to Mumfrey's beak. The beans looked a great deal like birdseed, and the quail was feeling irritable.

Harriet and the chipmunk both stared at the quail in dismay.

"Well, now you owe me a quail," said the chipmunk.

"Not happening," said Harriet. "And he only ate one bean, so technically I'd only owe you a third of a quail, even if I agreed to it, which I didn't."

"I'll give you the other two beans and take the quail!"

"The third bean is inside the quail, so you'd get both the bean *and* the quail, and I'd get nothing! If anything, you'd owe me another magic bean!"

The chipmunk clutched his ears. "But how am I supposed to get my bean back!?"

WELL, IF YOU WAIT ABOUT TWENTY-FOUR HOURS . . .

. . .

"Quails have a really fast digestion," said Harriet apologetically. "I mean, I'm sorry about your bean. He shouldn't have done that. But you still can't have Mumfrey."

The chipmunk stared at her.

"Look, would you take money? We can go to my dad's castle and I'm sure they'll pay you a fair price for your bean—"

The chipmunk let out a shriek of frustration and then, quite to Harriet's surprise, vanished in a puff of smoke.

... OKAY, THAT WAS WEIRD.

"I guess he was magical after all," said Harriet. "Hmm. Now I wonder about those beans . . ."

"Qwerk!" said Mumfrey, which is Quail for "I didn't like him at all." Then he belched.

"Jeez, Mumfrey!"

Harriet sighed. She was used to fairies and magical creatures that did weird things, but they didn't usually go *poof!* like that.

"Well," she said, "maybe he'll go to the castle. Mom and Dad will take care of it, I guess."

She gathered up Mumfrey's reins and they ambled down the road together.

MUMFREY!

CHAPTER 2

Harriet slept that night under the stars. She'd been meaning to go back home to the castle, but . . . well . . .

"Qwerrreeeeelllcch!"

"Mumfrey, I don't know what was in that bean you ate, but you smell like a rotten fish wrapped in old socks!"

Harriet wasn't the most princessly princess in the world—she was happy to admit that to anyone who would listen—but a good ruler takes care of the people she rules over. That meant that she didn't want to take Mumfrey to the castle stable and subject all the stable hands and the other quail and the kennel-newts to the extraordinary smells that Mumfrey was producing.

So she bedded down in a field, with Mumfrey downwind, and tried to sleep despite the noises that his innards were making. He sounded like bad plumbing.

"Good night, Mumfrey," she said. "Try to get some sleep."

In the morning, Harriet woke up feeling re-freshed. "Hey, it stopped smelling around here. Mumfrey! Do you feel better?"

"Qwerk!" said Mumfrey, which is Quail for "Much better!"

"What a great morning! I could go for a cup of tea . . ."

It was a beautiful morning. The sun was shining and the birds (other than Mumfrey) were singing. A little breeze blew, and went:

WHOMPH WHOMPH
SNAP WHOMPH
WHOMPH
SNAP WHOMPH

Harriet paused.

She was used to breezes going "whoosh" or perhaps "swish." She was not used to them making a sound like a gigantic tarp snapping in a gale.

"Uh . . . Mumfrey? Did you just hear . . . ?"

. . . QWERK?!

Harriet turned.

Behind their campsite, a gigantic beanstalk climbed into the heavens. The top was lost in the clouds.

The sound that Harriet had heard was the leaves moving in the breeze. Each leaf was the size of a barn roof, and when the wind moved them, where a normal bean plant would have gone *rustle-rustle,* the giant beanstalk went *WHOMPH WHOMPH WHOOOOOMPH.*

The trunk was as thick around as the tower that Harriet had lived in until the incident with the thorn hedge. There was a bean dangling a few stories up that could have fed an entire village for a week, and somebody could have lived in the empty bean pod afterward.

"Mumfrey," said Harriet slowly as her eyes went up . . . and up . . . and up . . . "Mumfrey, at some point last night, did you get up to use the bathroom?"

"Qwerk," muttered Mumfrey, scuffing his foot on the ground.

"I know that wasn't there yesterday," said Harriet. "But you ate a bean and now there's . . . that. So . . ."

"Qwerk!" said Mumfrey irritably. This is Quail for "Fine! Yes, well, everybody does it. And I felt better afterward."

Harriet could picture exactly what had happened.

The magic bean had emerged back into the world—ahem—and found itself in a pile of the highest-quality fertilizer that a trained battle quail could produce.

And it had grown.

It had grown a *lot*.

The breeze blew again and she saw the bean leaves lifting like sails in the wind. A cloud drifted away, and she saw even more of the beanstalk, going up and up, and then into another bank of clouds.

"Well," said Harriet. "I guess I owe that chipmunk an apology. Those really *were* magic beans."

CHAPTER 3

The beanstalk cast a shadow like a black bar, stretching for miles. People were going to start coming to investigate soon. Harriet didn't really want to have to explain things.

UH, YEAH,
SO MY QUAIL ATE THIS
MAGIC BEAN AND LOOK,
MISTAKES WERE MADE
AND . . . UM . . .

On the other hand, it was not very heroic to leave a giant beanstalk lying around, where it might present a threat to migrating birds and low-flying dragons and whatnot. And it was Mumfrey's fault, and that meant it was Harriet's fault, because she was Mumfrey's owner.

Harriet walked around the beanstalk. It was rigidly straight, which beanstalks usually weren't. She chalked that up to magic.

"Okay," she said. "So if I get an ax and chop this down, it's going to fall."

She looked around. In three directions there were trees, which would probably prefer not to be flattened. In the fourth direction, there was a farm field and off in the distance, a village.

If she chopped the beanstalk down, there was a chance it might land on the village.

This would be *very* bad. People would complain.

Her parents were pretty good about letting her wander around on her own having adventures, but there were limits. Accidentally flattening a village would definitely get her grounded, possibly for life.

"Hmmm . . ."

The leaves went *WHOOOSH*.

And then, very far away, as if from the top of the beanstalk, Harriet heard another sound. It was very thin and very faint and it sounded like . . .

IS THAT . . . HARP MUSIC?

"Who's playing a harp up on top of a giant plant?" asked Harriet.

"Qwerk," said Mumfrey, which is Quail for "No idea."

"Well, now I really can't chop it down if there's somebody on top of it!"

"Qwerk."

Harriet scowled. She stomped around. She built a small campfire and made tea. She stomped around some more, and then discovered that most of her tea had spilled out and she had to make more.

Carefully not stomping, she drank her tea and listened.

There is something very soothing about making tea. You have to concentrate on the whole process, and then you have tea. Even someone as decisive as Harriet had to make tea sometimes and think things through.

"Someone's up there," said Harriet. "And I suppose that means I have to go up and find out what's going on."

She placed her mug carefully in the ashes of the campfire, where it would stay warm.

"All right, Mumfrey," she said, cracking her knuckles. "Let's go."

CHAPTER 4

Battle quail, as everyone knows, cannot fly. They can shlop, which is a bizarre bouncing gait like a gallop with flapping. It is not dignified, but it gets the job done.

They can also glide very well.

If Harriet was climbing the beanstalk by herself and slipped, she would have only an instant to grab a handhold before she was engaged in a sudden, spectacular cliff-dive with no water at the bottom.

But if Mumfrey climbed the beanstalk, using his heavy claws, and he slipped, all he would have to do would be to spread his wings and glide safely to the ground.

Harriet was brave and strong and confident in her abilities, but she still would never have tried to climb the beanstalk without specialized equipment like ropes and crampons and spiked shoes . . . or a battle quail.

Up Mumfrey went, digging his clawed feet into the woody surface of the beanstalk. Occasionally he grabbed the base of a leaf in his bill and used it to haul himself up. All Harriet had to do was hang on tight and listen to the distant, elusive harp music.

"You're doing great!" she told him.

"Grrrnnggghwerk!" said Mumfrey, with his mouth full of leaves.

On they went, higher and higher.

Harriet looked down and saw the world spread out under her like a quilt. The forest made big green puffy patches, and the fields were brown and golden, and the village streets looked like lines of embroidery.

"Nice view," said Harriet.

It would probably look less nice if she'd dropped a beanstalk the size of a giant sequoia on it. She sighed.

It was cold in the upper reaches of the beanstalk. Harriet wished briefly that she was a fluffy teddy bear hamster. She pulled her arms inside her jacket and hunched her shoulders up around her ears.

Mumfrey pulled them up another few feet, and suddenly they were in the clouds.

It was soggy and foggy and cold. Harriet could barely see Mumfrey's bobbing topknot in front of her.

"Clouds," muttered Harriet. "They look so pretty and then you get into them and it's just a pile of fog."

Mumfrey qwerked irritably. He didn't like what fog did to his feathers.

They climbed inside the cloud for what felt like hours, but which was probably only about ten minutes. Mumfrey had to set his feet carefully on the damp beanstalk.

Harriet knew that this was the most dangerous

part of the climb. It was so cold and the air was so thin that if Mumfrey fell and tried to fly, his wings might ice. Then it wouldn't matter if he could fly.

Suddenly they broke through the surface of the cloud.

"Whoa," said Harriet. "Now THIS is gonna be a problem."

CHAPTER 5

There was a castle in the clouds.

There's nothing inherently wrong with having a castle in the clouds, of course. You don't have to worry about the neighbors, for one thing, and if you run out of space, you can always find a nice chunk of cumulus somewhere, attach a grappling hook, and add a wing on the castle that way.

The downside is that if you're drifting along without a care in the world, you run the chance of becoming hung up on, for example, a giant beanstalk that someone has carelessly left lying around.

Harriet stepped cautiously off onto the clouds. She kept hold of Mumfrey's saddle, in case the clouds weren't quite solid, but her feet sank in and then stopped. It was like walking on marshmallow.

"Well," said Harriet gloomily, "I suppose we have to go in and apologize to the owner of the castle for having hooked their cloud."

"Qwerk," said Mumfrey, which is Quail for "This would be the civic-minded thing to do."

They approached the castle.

Indeed, they approached the castle for rather longer than Harriet expected. She had thought it was very close, but eventually she realized that it was enormous and fairly far away. The sounds of the harp came to them in snatches on the wind.

Once they finally reached the castle, it seemed . . . crude. You still had to call it a castle—anything that size was *definitely* a castle—but the door was made of rough logs. The stones were thrown together with globs of mortar between them. It looked more like a giant cabin than like the castle that Harriet had grown up in.

It went up for what seemed like miles. Whoever lived in the castle was very large indeed.

"An Ogrecat could live here," said Harriet. "Or a dragon. A *big* dragon. Or a giant."

"Qwerk."

Harriet sighed. Very large people were not inherently evil, of course, any more than regular-sized people, but dragons and Ogrecats were carnivorous and sometimes they tried to dine on hamster. Everyone in the kingdom knew better than to mess with Princess Harriet, but it was possible that the word hadn't gotten up into the clouds yet.

She didn't mind having to fight monsters—she rather enjoyed it—but it seemed kind of rude to snag someone's castle and then beat them up.

"It'd be entrapment or something," she said to Mumfrey. "Probably."

She knocked on the massive door.

Even though she banged her knuckles against the wood as hard as she could, the sound seemed tiny. Would they even hear her?

KNOCK!
KNOCK!
KNOCK!

She lifted her paw to knock again. Nothing happened.

Mumfrey cleared his throat and pointed with a wing.

There was a gap in the door where the hinges joined the wall. It was a very small gap compared to the size of the door, but a very large gap if you were a hamster.

Harriet stepped through. Mumfrey sucked in his gut and followed her.

The harp music was suddenly much louder. It was definitely coming from inside the castle.

"Hello?" called Harriet. "Is anybody there?"

She poked her head around the door, one hand on the hilt of her sword.

The room was huge, cavernous, the ceiling so high that it was almost lost in shadow. The beams overhead were whole tree trunks, with bark still on them. Harriet saw a bent nail in the door that was longer than she was tall.

The music stopped.

CHAPTER 6

She heard a soft shuffling in the far reaches of the room. "Who's there?"

"Me," said Harriet. "Princess Harriet Hamsterbone."

"Are you a friend of the giant?"

It was a female voice, and sounded young. Harriet peered into the gloom and saw movement, high up on the wall. "No," she said. "I mean, not that I'm his enemy either. We've never met."

"You'll probably want to keep it that way," said the voice. "He's not a nice sort. Eats people."

Harriet sighed. "I was afraid of that. It always ends in cannibalism."

Mumfrey looked nervously over his wing. A people-eating cloud giant?

"If you leave now, you'll probably get away," said the voice. "He's off hunting storms."

"Storms?" said Harriet, stepping farther into the room.

"He's a storm hunter. A good storm can fetch a high price on the open market. That's how he bought me." There was an odd, discordant noise, like somebody had banged a harp string in annoyance.

BOUGHT YOU? WHAT?

She did *not* approve of people being bought. Or sold, for that matter. Once you started treating people like things you could buy and sell, you were firmly on the Bad Guy side of the equation. (Eating people was also bad, of course, but monsters did have to eat, so the trick was to get them into things like tofu and carrots that didn't object to being eaten.) She wondered if the giant would like to eat beans. There had to be plenty on the vine for even the biggest giant.

"Bought," said the voice, and a sad arpeggio drifted from the back of the room, followed by another discordant twang.

"Are you playing the harp back there?" asked Harriet.

"In a manner of speaking," said the voice. "I strongly suggest you run away now, but if you're staying, come a little closer. I'm up on a shelf and it's hard to get down."

Harriet strode out into the room.

She strode boldly, because she was Harriet Hamsterbone, princess, warrior, bane of evil witches and unreasonable kings. But she still felt like an insect crossing the floor.

Everything was just so *large*. There was a giant chair ahead of her, and looking up the legs was like looking up in a forest.

The giant had to be thirty feet tall, to use a chair like that. A thirty-foot giant that ate people. This was shaping up to be a lovely day.

She skirted the chair and an even larger table. There was a fireplace on one wall. Harriet's entire bedroom would fit in that fireplace. An old-fashioned oil lamp on the table had a glass dome over it the size of a greenhouse and there were a couple of shelves on the walls and a door.

Other than that, there was almost no furniture. The room seemed very bare. For all that it looked like a castle to Harriet, to a giant it might be a rather small cabin.

"You don't seem to be running away," said the voice.

"I'm very brave," said Harriet, because it was true. "My friend Wilbur would add 'and not always bright' at this point, but he's not here, so let's not worry about that."

The shelf was so far up the wall that she could only see the bottom. There was a thump and another twang of music, and a face came into view.

"You're a hamster!" said Harriet, delighted.

"Close, but not quite," said the stranger. "I'm a harpster. My name's Strings."

"Harpster?"

Strings rested her chin on her hands. "It's easier to explain if you come up here."

Harriet looked around. There were no ladders, no ropes, nothing up the wall. Except . . .

"Aha!"

The giant chair had a back like a ladder. Harriet climbed onto Mumfrey's back. "Up, Mumfrey!"

"Qwerk?" muttered Mumfrey, which is Quail for "Why am I doing all the work here?"

But he hopped up the leg of the chair, digging his claws into the wood, and then up onto the seat. Harriet stood up in the saddle and jumped for the first slat on the back of the chair. She caught it and began to climb.

Strings nodded. "I figured your bird would fly up," she said. "But that works too."

"Mumfrey has a lot of talents," said Harriet. "Sustained flight isn't one of them. He is a top-notch battle quail, though!"

She reached the top of the chair and eyed the gap.

It was a big jump for a
hamster, which is not, by
nature, a species given to
leaping.

But Harriet was used to cliff-diving, which starts with a jump, and landed easily.

"Whoa!" said Strings.

". . . whoa," said Harriet.

They gazed at each other in frank amazement.

Harpster.

Strings was, in fact, a hamster . . . from the front.

From the back, she was a harp.

CHAPTER 7

You're a harp!" said Harriet.

"No," said Strings, "I'm a harpster. Half hamster, half harp. It's complicated."

"I can see how it might be," said Harriet.

Strings shrugged. Her shoulders went up and the strings rippled behind her, a complicated scale that still *sounded* like a shrug.

"So you live here with the giant?"

Strings gave her a sarcastic look. "Well, I can't exactly leave," she said.

"You can't?" asked Harriet.

The harp rolled her eyes and turned slightly, so that Harriet could see a shackle running around the back of the harp, attached to a long chain. "I'm not here for my health."

Harriet scowled. "I *see*." She'd suspected as much, given the whole *bought* thing, but it was infuriating to see it. She decided right then that she wasn't leaving without taking Strings with her.

Strings turned and walked along the line of the shelf. Her legs were fused to the body of the harp, and she could only move in small, shuffling steps. The links of the chain clinked as she moved.

"He doesn't mistreat me or anything. I mean, other than not letting me leave. But he's so *boring*. He wants the same music over and over." She picked out an arpeggio on the strings. It sounded beautiful to Harriet, if you liked that sort of thing.

"Plunk, plunk, wordless lullaby, plinka plunk. I'm really suffering creatively here."

She slapped the strings with one hand, fist raised. The noise that came out sounded raw and angry, like thunder.

"Wow," said Harriet. "I didn't know a harp could *make* a sound like that!"

"Most of them can't," said Strings. "I have to clench a lot of muscles. I have *amazing* abs."

"Cool!" said Harriet. She'd always wanted to be in a band. "Do you need a drummer?"

"Maybe," said the harp. "What are your qualifications?"

"I can hit things really hard and my arms don't get tired."

"Okay, you're in."

Harriet opened her mouth to ask another question, when a horrific cackling came from the dark corner by the fireplace.

"Yikes!" said Harriet. "What was that?"

"That's the goose," said Strings. "My fellow captive. Doesn't sing very well, I'm afraid. She's a softy. Lays eggs."

"Golden eggs?" asked Harriet, who knew how these things usually go.

Strings stared at her blankly. "Brown," she said. "He eats them for breakfast. And lunch and sometimes dinner. And he puts so much chili powder on them, it'll make you sneeze."

RIGHT, RIGHT.
SORRY. YOU START CLIMBING
BEANSTALKS, AND YOU GET THESE
WEIRD IDEAS. MUST BE THE
ALTITUDE.

"The goose is okay," said Strings. "She comes up occasionally and I scratch her beak."

Harriet nodded. Mumfrey also liked to have his beak scratched, right around the base, where things got itchy.

Mumfrey hopped down from the chair and went to go investigate the goose. Harriet heard a "Qwerk!" and a "Honk!" and then the chatty "squonk-chrrk-blat" noises of two birds getting acquainted.

"She does lay eggs when she gets nervous. Sort of spontaneously. It's a bit awkward."

Harriet had recently had to lug a hydra egg around on her back. The hydra was half the size of a goose. She tried to imagine the size of the eggs that the goose might lay, and made a note to stay well clear of the bird's back end.

"So the giant bought you," said Harriet. "How? From where?"

Strings scowled. "I was stupid. I went to talk to what I thought was a music agent. Someone to set up tours and book castles to play at and whatnot. And instead he stuffed me in a sack and sold me off to a giant!"

"That jerk!"

"I know, right?!" Strings waved her arms in the air. Her strings jangled furiously. Harriet wondered if they ever snapped, and if so, if it was painful.

"Does your family know where you are?"

The harpster shook her head. "Don't really have one. A wizard made a couple of us one day, as an experiment. I mean, he was very nice about it. Made sure we had a proper education and let us go off and follow our dreams. My . . . sister, I guess . . . is a harpsterichord and plays in a monastery. She seems happy. But I wanted to go out and do things! See the world! Shake the dust of that wizard's laboratory off my tuning pins!"

BUT THEN, Y'KNOW. GIANT.

Harriet could sympathize. She herself had wanted to get out of her parents' castle and explore the world as soon as she was old enough to toddle down to the stable and climb on a quail's back.

"Anyway," said Strings, "it was great to meet you, and if I ever escape, I will look you up for Ironstring. But you really ought to leave before the giant gets back."

"I'm going to help you escape," said Harriet.

Strings gave her a skeptical look. "Are you sure? Did I mention that he's about thirty feet tall? And eats people?"

"Trust me," said Harriet. "I'm a professional."

And no sooner had she said that than the door was flung open and a vast roaring voice shouted, "I'm home!"

CHAPTER 8

Strings grabbed Harriet's hand and pulled her toward the back of the shelf. There was a pile of straw padded with what looked like giant towels.

"Hide!" hissed Strings. "The goose will take care of Mumfrey!"

Harriet hoped that the harpster was right. She dove under one of the towels and tried to look like straw.

The giant closed the door. Under the edge of

the towel, Harriet could see the enormous shape stomp across the floor, drop his bag (his bag was bigger than a wagon) on the floor . . . and pause.

The giant turned toward the back of the room. He had incredibly long ears, dangling past his belt, and was wearing boots so enormous that a regular-sized person could have put a roof over one and set up house.

Rabbit, thought Harriet. *Giant Lop, I think, which would make sense. Problem is that once they get to this size, they stop wanting to eat just vegetables . . .*

"I smell something!" roared the giant rabbit. "Harp, has someone been here?"

"My name isn't Harp," said Strings.

The giant ignored her. "Fee fie foe . . . uh . . . famster," he said. "I smell the blood of a mortal hamster!"

"Famster?" said Harriet under her breath. "*Famster? Seriously? Oh, now it's on.*" As a princess, she expected to have a certain amount of bad poetry written about her, but there were limits.

"Yes, yes," said Strings. "There *was* a hamster."

Harriet held her breath. Had she misjudged the harpster? Was Strings about to reveal her to the giant?

SHE LEFT BEFORE YOU CAME BACK.

An expression of alarm crossed the giant's face. "Did she steal my treasure?"

"Well, I'm still here," said Strings.

"Not *you,*" said the giant rudely, and stomped over to the doorway on the far side of the room.

Harriet caught a glimpse of an enormous bed through the door and an equally enormous chest. The giant opened the chest and began digging through it.

"Oh, thanks," muttered Strings. "Nice to know that I'm valued. Bad enough to get bought and sold, but to someone who doesn't care that you exist . . ."

She plucked a bitter arpeggio.

"Should we make a break for it?" whispered Harriet.

"No," whispered Strings, over the notes. "He'll go to sleep after dinner. That's the best time."

"Got it."

Harriet settled down to wait. She hoped that Mumfrey was doing the same, and that the goose could keep him safe.

Mumfrey, for his part, was tucked up underneath the goose like a chick under its mother. While most people would object to being sat on by a giant goose, for a bird like Mumfrey, this was actually quite comfortable. It reminded him of being a very young quail, when he and his sisters had snuggled up under his mother's wings at night. There were several eggs under there with him, and they were warm and smooth and comfortable.

He was, in fact, starting to fall asleep.

ZZZZ

He was about to have a very rude awakening.

The giant left his bedroom, apparently satisfied. "Next time, try to keep the hamster here," he ordered Strings.

"How do you know I didn't?" asked the harpster. "You got in late."

"Yes, well . . ."

SOME IDIOT LEFT A GIANT BEANSTALK LYING AROUND, AND WE'VE SNAGGED ON IT.

"So cut us loose," said Strings.

The giant groaned. "It'll be two days with an ax," he said. "The cloud's all tangled up and I'll have to chop all the tangled bits free. Clouds are delicate, you know."

He built up the fire. The logs beside the fireplace were whole trees. The fire roared, and he took down a frying pan as big as Harriet's bed and slid it over the fire.

Then he casually reached over and shoved his hand underneath the goose.

The goose honked in alarm. Strings put her hands over her mouth.

Harriet cringed.

The giant pulled out one egg, two eggs, and then—

"What's this?" cried the giant.

He yanked his hand free of the traumatized goose.

CHAPTER 9

"Fee fie foe fear!" cried the giant. "How did a quail get in here?"

Mumfrey squawked and flailed in the giant rabbit's fist, to no avail. The goose honked wildly, then made a strangled sound. An egg plopped out and rolled along the floor, going *wogga wogga wogga* as it teetered in a circle.

Harriet lunged forward instinctively, reaching for her sword. She had to save Mumfrey!

Strings sidestepped, pulled the chain holding

her taut, and tripped Harriet with it. The hamster landed flat on her face.

"Not now!" hissed Strings in her ear. "You'll get yourself eaten!"

WE'VE GOT TO WAIT UNTIL HE'S ASLEEP!

Harriet gritted her teeth, but she knew Strings was right. She didn't dare attack the giant right now. Not while he had Mumfrey actually in his hand and could squish her poor battle quail in an instant!

She crawled backward, into the nest of towels, seething.

"Well," said the giant, who had been too busy

studying Mumfrey to notice what was happening on the shelf behind him. "Well, well. It's a quail. What are you doing here, little bird?"

He finally turned and looked at Strings. "And why didn't you mention it?"

"Thought it had left," said Strings nonchalantly. "The hamster came in with it. Left with it too. It must have come back to see the goose."

"And you didn't hear it come in?" asked the giant suspiciously.

"I take naps sometimes, you know," said the harpster. "It's pretty boring here. I mean, would it kill you to bring some reading material back sometime? A couple of books, or a magazine?"

The giant turned back to Mumfrey. "Well, good luck for me, anyway. I'll have a quail omelet tonight!"

Harriet dug her fingernails into the wooden

shelf hard enough to get splinters. If he tried to eat Mumfrey, she was going to run out there and stab him in the ankle, giant or no giant!

Strings gulped and looked over her shoulder at Harriet's hiding place. Harriet saw an expression of panic pass over the harpster's face.

Then she squared her shoulders (the strings went *jingle-jangle* as she did so) and turned back.

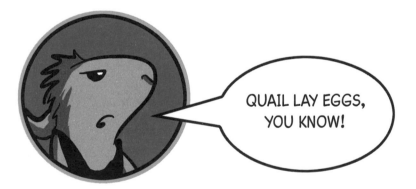

QUAIL LAY EGGS, YOU KNOW!

The giant paused, with Mumfrey still in his fist. "What?"

"They're birds," she said. "They lay eggs."

Mumfrey looked faintly insulted. While some male birds did occasionally get confused and lay eggs, nobody in his family had ever done anything so crass.

Fortunately for him, it's very difficult to tell male and female quail apart, unless you're a quail yourself.

"I'm just saying," said Strings, "that you can eat the quail tonight, or you can have quail eggs in your omelets for days to come. You've got to be bored with goose eggs by now."

The giant visibly wavered. "Won't they be tiny?"

"I hear they're a delicacy in some places." (This is actually true. Mumfrey had made it clear to Harriet that he did not want to visit those places. He didn't mind people eating eggs, but there's something weird about seeing them eat eggs from your own species.)

"No sense eating the quail that lays the . . . err . . . tasty eggs," said Strings, examining her nails.

"You're pretty smart for a harp," said the giant slowly. "That's a good idea. And if I don't like the eggs, I can always eat the quail later!"

"Qwerk!" said Mumfrey, trying hard to look like a quail who would lay absolutely delicious eggs.

The giant opened a cupboard and pulled out a wooden cage. It looked small in the enormous rabbit's hand. He popped the top open and dropped Mumfrey inside.

Then he set the cage on the mantel of the fireplace, twenty feet off the ground.

Harriet narrowed her eyes. How was she going to get Mumfrey down now?

The giant picked up the spontaneously laid egg, then crouched down in front of the fireplace and cracked the goose eggs into the frying pan. He pulled a sack out of the cupboard and dumped it over the eggs. For a minute Harriet thought it was spices, and then she realized that the giant was dumping an entire sack of potatoes into the pan.

The scale is starting to get to me, she thought. *When I go back down the beanstalk, everything is going to look tiny. Like a dollhouse.* (Harriet had owned a dollhouse when she was young, because her mother thought that dollhouses were the sort of thing a princess should own. This lasted until she discovered Harriet using her dolls to play Invading Army, where the heroic defenders of the dollhouse stood off a siege by the attackers, and occasionally threw the attackers off the roof. Her mother had been horrified and the dollhouse had been banished to the attic.)

She itched to do something, but all she could do was settle in to wait until the giant finished his dinner and finally went to bed.

CHAPTER 10

Fortunately it didn't take long. The giant finished his meal, belched loudly, and then dumped grain for the goose into a food dish labeled GOOSEY.

"Does he feed you?" Harriet whispered.

"I'm an enchanted harp," said Strings. "I don't have a digestive system. I live on the joyous spirit of music or something like that. The wizard had a sentimental streak."

"Eh?" said the giant, turning his head.

"Nothing," said Strings.

The giant grunted. Harriet was starting to think that his hearing wasn't very good, despite those gigantic ears.

The giant glanced up at Mumfrey, then plopped a potato into his cage. Mumfrey gazed at it sadly.

"Qwweeerrr-eerk . . ." he said, which is Quail for "I have the quailhouse blues and I don't even have a harmonica." (The quailhouse blues are like the jailhouse blues, only for birds.)

"Eat up, birdy!" said the giant. "I'm gonna want eggs!"

He banked the fire and turned down the lamp,

yawning. "All right, Harp. Play me one of those lullabies. You know the kind I like."

Strings rolled her eyes but didn't say anything. She reached her arms back and began to run her fingers over the strings of her harp half.

The sound that emerged was slow and liquid. It flowed through the room like water, and seemed to say *Sleep . . . Sleep . . .*

Even Harriet found herself yawning.

Sleep . . . Sleep . . .

"Of course, that won't work on me," Harriet said to herself. "I'm a seasoned warrior . . . zz . . . zzzz . . ."

She was astonished when, a few minutes later, Strings was shaking her awake.

"Whoa," Harriet said. "What happened?"

"It's a pretty serious lullaby," said the harpster. "Has to be, to put out a giant. He's gone to bed."

"Right." Harriet sat up, covering her mouth with her hand, and yawned again. "Right. Okay."

"Give him an hour," warned Strings. "He wakes up easily at first. Wait until he's snoring."

Harriet nodded.

She took the time to sit down and compose a letter home to her parents. She had no idea how she would mail it, but she always tried to write home before a pitched battle, just so that her mom wouldn't worry.

Dear Mom & Dad,

I am sorry that I will not be home for dinner. There was an inconvenient beanstalk. It is not too large, only a mile or so high. Also, there is a giant. He is much smaller than the beanstalk, but wicked. The beanstalk is not wicked, so far as I know. I am not sure how

beanstalks would be wicked. Dad would not like it, though. I know how he feels about very large plants, after the thorn hedge incident. I may have to fight the giant.

I have made a friend named Strings who is a harpster . . .

She finished the letter and read it over. Then she tried to read it again, as if she were Wilbur. After a minute, she added:

Don't worry. I will be fine and probably won't get squashed. Love, Harriet.

That didn't seem to be quite enough.

She wrote:

P.S. I have fought giants before, so I am sure it will be okay.

She put the letter away, frowning. She hoped that it was true. The giant was extremely large, and Harriet hadn't actually fought a giant since she had stopped being invincible. Being invincible wasn't everything, but it counted for a lot when you were up against a foe that big.

The more she thought about it, the more she hoped that she could get everyone out without fighting the giant. Brave warriors were all very good, but *smart* warriors lived a lot longer and got to show their medals to their grandkids.

A noise echoed through the castle. It sounded like a cross between a lonely whale and an erupting volcano.

Harriet blinked.

"I know, right?" said Strings.

Harriet shook her head, amazed. She'd heard some pretty brutal snoring in her life, but that was something else entirely.

"Well, then." She rubbed her hands together. "Let's get us all out of here."

CHAPTER 11

This was easier said than done. Harriet walked the length of the shelf, studying the room. The bedroom door was ajar, and she could hear the giant snoring. Even the goose, curled up by the fire, was honking quietly in her sleep.

Mumfrey, in the cage on the mantel, looked at Harriet sadly. He was still awake.

"Qwerk," he sighed.

Harriet waved to him and surveyed the rest of the room. Finally she turned back to Strings.

"Can you jump?"

Strings pushed off with her toes and managed a two-inch hop.

"Err. How *high* can you jump?"

"You're looking at it," said Strings. "These legs are mostly decorative carvings."

"Right," said Harriet. "New plan. Can you climb a rope?"

"No problem," said Strings. "You try playing the harp backward your whole life, you'll get biceps like you wouldn't believe."

GREAT!
WE'LL CLIMB DOWN.

She'd actually seen something that could be used as a rope earlier. The hard part was going to be getting to it.

"What happens once we get down?" asked Strings. She folded her arms. "Because if you're expecting me to make a run for the door, you'd better have an hour or so free."

"Do you think you can ride Mumfrey?"

Strings tapped her fingernail against her front teeth. "Hmmm. It'd be awkward, but yes, I think so. If we run a rope through here"—she waved toward the opening with the strings in her harp half—"and tie me into the saddle . . . yeah."

"Might be pretty uncomfortable," warned Harriet. Being tied to the saddle of a galloping quail wasn't high on anyone's list of a great time.

"Oh, I'll be terribly out of tune by the end, I'm sure." Strings shrugged.

CAN'T BE MORE UNCOMFORTABLE THAN BEING A PRISONER IN A GIANT'S CASTLE, CAN IT?

"Probably not," said Harriet. "All right." She looked across the room to where Mumfrey sat sadly in his cage.

"How do you plan to get him down?" asked Strings.

"I haven't got the foggiest idea," said Harriet. "But don't worry. I'll think of something. I always do."

Fortunately, the giant hadn't pushed his chair in when he got up from the table. Harriet wasn't sure how she would have moved it back into position. It had to weigh at least a thousand pounds. But it was in more or less the same place, only a little bit farther away from the shelf.

She leaped from the shelf to the chair and swung down. In the cage overhead, Mumfrey qwerked worriedly at her.

Harriet didn't dare shout up to him, but she waved reassuringly. He looked more dejected than she'd ever seen him.

"I'll get you out, buddy, I promise," she muttered. "You and Strings—and the goose too!"

It wasn't as easy getting down from the chair without a quail to help. Harriet had to dig her fingers into the rough wood of the chair leg. She had acquired a truly heroic set of splinters by the time she reached the bottom.

"Ow," she mumbled, pulling one out with her teeth. "'At 'urts!"

She crossed the wooden floor to the back wall. The giant had left the door just slightly ajar—but slightly ajar for a giant was still enormous. Harriet stepped through without even having to turn sideways.

The giant's bedroom was dark except for the red glow of the fire behind her. Harriet paused to let her eyes adjust.

The enormous rabbit was covered by acres of quilts. His mouth hung open and the snores poured out of it.

Harriet looked around. An idea had been poking at the back of her mind ever since she'd seen the giant stomping through the room.

"Now where are his shoes . . . ?"

She scanned the floor, increasingly puzzled. There was the bed, which sat directly on the floor with no space under it. There was a big chest that practically screamed "Treasure Goes Here!" which was of no particular interest to Harriet. You started digging around in treasure chests and you always got caught. It was practically the law.

Besides, her father already owned a kingdom. There was no point in getting greedy.

Other than the chest, there was nothing. The giant didn't even have a nightstand with a glass of water.

"His shoes have to be somewhere . . ." muttered Harriet to herself.

She inched farther into the room.

The giant let out another snore and rolled over. Harriet flattened herself against the wall.

And then she saw it.

When the Giant Lop rolled over, he stuck one of his feet out from under the covers. (Harriet also liked to sleep with one foot out from under the covers herself, so she quite understood this.)

The giant was wearing his shoes in bed.

Harriet gazed up at the enormous foot, in the equally enormous shoe. Holding it together, the ends trailing untidily, was a shoelace.

The shoelace was as long and thick as any rope that Harriet had ever seen. She just had to get it out of the shoe.

Which would have been a lot easier if he didn't sleep with his shoes on, she thought grimly.

She rubbed her hands together. In the room behind her, between the snores, she heard Mumfrey quietly crooning the quailhouse blues.

(". . . qwerka-qwerk-werk-werka-qwerk . . .")

"Right," she said to herself. "Let's do this thing."

CHAPTER 12

Getting up on the bed was relatively easy. The blankets fell over the edge to the floor, and Harriet could literally walk right up them. She went to the foot of the bed, and started her hike.

The valiant Princess Harriet ascends Mount Giant! she thought. *The valiant Princess Harriet is a third of the way up!*

The giant snored.

Now halfway . . . now three-fifths . . .

(". . . qwerka-werk, qwerka-werrrrrk . . .")

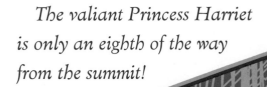

The valiant Princess Harriet is only an eighth of the way from the summit!

The giant went *"SNRRRGHHHKK!"* and turned his head on the pillow. Harriet had to clutch at the blankets as the whole bed shook.

Her weight was negligible compared to the enormous blankets, but she still pulled a fold more tightly over the giant's ankle.

"Mnnghhk," he mumbled, and flexed his foot.

Harriet saw the sole of the shoe coming toward her like a wall. She flung herself flat, digging into the blankets, as the giant's foot passed over her head with barely an inch to spare.

She rolled over on her back and grabbed for the shoe before it could come back the other way and possibly squish her. The shoelaces were enormous and crisscrossed like a rope ladder. Harriet jammed her arm in between the laces and hauled herself up.

It took several minutes for the giant to settle, during which time Harriet grimly rode the foot back and forth.

Every time he flexed his toes, her teeth rattled in her head.

(Hamsters, like many rodents, have teeth that grow their entire lives, so Harriet wasn't all that worried about breaking one. It would grow back, it just would have been annoying. And if one tooth broke, the other one often grew in lopsided, and she'd be spending hours with a steel file trying to get it evened out.)

Eventually, the giant let out a truly epic snore and his foot relaxed. Harriet climbed to the top of the foot.

The valiant Princess Harriet reaches the top of Mount Giant!

The shoelaces were a knotted mess, and they stank. They smelled like feet and like shoes that somebody has been wearing for years without any socks. It was nasty.

The laces had absorbed all that funk. Some of the knots were as big as she was. Possibly the giant didn't take his shoes off to sleep because he couldn't get them untied.

Harriet sighed.

If she'd had her sword, she could have sawed through the laces, but it was in Mumfrey's pack.

That only left one option.

"If there was a rope anywhere else in this castle…!" she muttered to herself.

She took a deep breath, which was a mistake, because then she got a lungful of foot smell. She stifled a cough, let it out, and took a very shallow breath.

Then she scrunched up her face, set her chisel-like hamster teeth against the shoelace, and began to gnaw.

CHAPTER 13

It tasted *awful*.
The shoelaces parted easily under her teeth, but she had to keep stopping because the taste was so unspeakably nasty.

It was like . . . like . . . well, Harriet didn't know how to describe what it was like. It seemed like

you'd need epic poetry to do justice to a taste like this. Her parents had hired a tutor to teach her poetry, that being one of the princessly arts, but he had wanted her to recite poems about clouds and flowers, and Harriet was more interested in poems about mighty adventures and glorious final charges into battle.

"I sing of the hero Harriet, quail-rider, fighter of foot funk . . . No, just doesn't have the same ring to it. . . ."

She sighed and went back to chewing on the shoelace.

Eventually—after Harriet had to stop several times to gag quietly into her elbow—the shoelace parted. The enormous knot at the top tumbled off the shoe and fell to the floor. It landed with a thump.

Harriet clung to the top of the shoe, waiting

to see if the sound had woken its owner. She was glad that she hadn't had anything more than tea since the night before. If there had been anything in her stomach, she'd probably lose it loudly, and there's nothing worse than trying to fight a giant while you have the dry heaves.

The giant didn't stir.

Great. Now I just need to get this unlaced . . . somehow . . .

She grabbed one end of the shoelace and began to feed it through the hole in the leather.

The lace came out easily, but there was a *lot*

of it. She stopped to wipe her face and without warning, the giant rolled over.

For a brief moment, up was down and down was up and Harriet was dangling over empty space.

She had the shoelace wrapped around one arm, so she didn't fall very far. But she hit the end of the lace with a squeak and hung there, spinning slowly.

Does he know I'm here? Can he feel me?

Let's see, if I'm one-thirtieth his size, then something one-thirtieth my size would be about the size of a small sack of flour. If a sack of flour was hanging off my foot, I'd feel it!

She had to get off his foot before he woke the rest of the way up.

"*Gnnnrrff . . .*" mumbled the giant. He reached an enormous hand down and scratched his ankle.

Harriet watched the hand coming and felt her heart pounding.

*He's just got an itch, he'll scratch
and then finish shortly, that's all—*

He didn't. He scratched harder.
The shoelace flopped back
and forth with Harriet
on the end.

WOGGA
WOGGA
WOGGA

"Hrrrzzzggh . . .
fuh . . . itchy . . ."
mumbled the giant.

*Oh no! That was a word!
He's waking up!*

"Feee . . . zzzz . . . foe . . . fitchy . . . footzzzz . . .
so . . . itchy . . ."

Harriet's heart hammered in her chest. She
had to get off the shoe, but not without the
shoelace!

She swung as hard as she could on the lace. It
was almost completely out of the shoe now.

It's at least 98/100ths of the way out—which re-
duces to 49/50ths, which doesn't reduce any further—

She was thinking this when the shoelace came 50/50ths of the way out of the shoe, which reduced all the way to 1, which reduced to Harriet falling toward the floor.

CHAPTER 14

She landed on the pile of knots that she had chewed free. It was slightly softer than landing on, say, sharp rocks, but not by much. Harriet lay across the pile of ropes for a minute, the breath knocked out of her. The shoelace landed across her back an instant later, so that it was like getting hit twice, once from below and once from above.

On the bed, the giant finally stopped scratching and went mumbling back to sleep.

Harriet concentrated on trying to get her breath

back. Unfortunately, since she was lying in a pile of concentrated foot funk, breathing wasn't that much better than not-breathing.

"Ungh," she said finally, pushing herself up. She pulled her shirt collar over her nose and began coiling the shoelace over her shoulder.

She felt exhausted. She'd fought Ogrecats and they hadn't been half so difficult.

Carrying the rope, and trying to breathe through her mouth—the shirt didn't help much— she staggered out of the room.

She made one detour on the way back to Strings. The goose was asleep with her head under her wing. In addition to the food bowl, she had a second bowl of water.

Harriet fell to her knees and dunked her entire head in it.

Eventually she had to come up for air. Her mouth felt better. Instead of tasting like feet, it tasted like water, and faintly like feathers. She could handle that. You didn't spend all day with a battle quail without getting used to feathers in your food.

Harriet climbed up the chair and leaped to the shelf, carrying the shoelace around her shoulder.

"Yeck," said Strings. "You're all wet. And what's that *smell?*"

"Giant shoelaces," said Harriet. "His feet have a giant funk to go with them. I don't think he ever takes them off."

"Shoelaces!" said Strings. "Of course!" She smacked her forehead with a jangling sound.

Harriet went to the back of the shelf. There was a gap between the giant board and the wall where Strings's chain dangled down. It was only about a foot wide, but that was more than enough space for Harriet. She fed the shoelace down around one of the shelf supports and began anchoring it in place.

"I just wonder why he wears shoes at all," she said as she worked.

"Oh, that's easy," said Strings. "It's clouds. You walk around on clouds all day, your feet get super-soggy. And giants have notoriously weak ankles."

"They do?"

"Yeah," said Strings. "They're carrying a lot of weight around. They all wind up wearing orthopedic shoes eventually."

"How do you know so much about giant feet?"

WHEN PRACTICALLY EVERYBODY ELSE IN THE WORLD HAS LEGS, YOU FIGURE THINGS OUT QUICK.

"Fascinating," said Harriet. "I shall keep this in mind the next time I fight a giant." She had finished tying the shoelace to the shelf support and began to feed it down over the edge. "Now let's see about this chain . . ."

"It's fastened to a hook on the wall down there," said Strings. "You'll have to actually get down to the hook to get it loose, though. I've tried everything from up here."

Harriet nodded. She'd only known Strings for a couple of hours, but it was pretty obvious that if there was an easy way to get free, the harpster would have done it already.

Harriet respected a kindred spirit, even if they were a magical musical instrument.

She grabbed the shoelace and jumped to the chair back. She could see the hook, gleaming red in the firelight. It was several yards beneath the shelf.

"Okay," she muttered. "Just like a rope swing back home . . ."

She wrapped her legs around the shoelace, grabbed with both hands, and pushed off from the chair.

WHEEEEEEEE!

CHAPTER 15

At first Harriet was afraid she wasn't going to get close enough to the hook, and then she was afraid she was going to get much *too* close. The hook had a wicked, backward-curving point, perfect for (to take an example completely and totally at random) impaling anybody who was swinging toward it at high speed on a giant shoelace.

"Uh-oh—"

She flung her weight sideways. The shoelace shuddered and the room swung dizzyingly. Unfortunately, she could still see the gleam of light off the point of the hook, which was still coming right at her.

"—uh-oh-uh-oh-uh-oh—"

If she got impaled on a hook in a strange castle, her mom was going to have a fit. Harriet let go with one hand and prepared to jump.

She hit the wall six inches from the hook, smashed her nose, nearly lost her grip on the shoelace, flailed wildly to catch it—and grabbed the chain. There was a jangle overhead as her weight struck the chain and yanked Strings over backward.

"You're telling me . . ." said Strings. The harpster sounded somewhat squashed.

The shoelace began trying to swing backward. Harriet clung to the chain. The chain slid downward, dragging Strings back across the shelf.

"Stop pulling!" cried Strings.

"Stop moving!" cried Harriet.

"I can't! There's nothing to grab!"

TWANG THUD
JANGLE-JANGLE-JANGLE

The chain slithered downward. So did Harriet. The shoelace burned through her fingers.

"Sorry!" said Harriet. She hadn't expected to drag Strings all the way across the shelf by the chain.

"It's fine," said Strings, obviously through gritted teeth. "Just—*hurry*."

Harriet climbed up the chain. Every time she grabbed a link, there was a grunt from overhead, as Strings took not only Harriet's weight, but the not-inconsiderable heft of the giant shoelace.

When she reached the hook, she grabbed it with both hands and took her weight off the chain at last.

"Oh, thank the myriad melodious gods of music," panted Strings.

Harriet's hands were starting to ache. She wished she'd brought gloves.

Fortunately, with the chain dangling so far down, it was easy. She gripped with one hand and unhooked the chain with the other. "There!" she said. "It's loose!"

Strings began to pull the chain up. Harriet watched as the last link vanished through the crack between shelf and wall.

"Come on, then," said Strings. "Let's get out of this place. I don't want to stay here one minute longer than I have to."

CHAPTER 16

In the end, it was harder than that, of course. Harriet had to perform some extraordinary contortions to get firmly back on the shoelace-rope, while still keeping hold of the hook. Her palms were burning and red by the time she managed to swing back over to the chair.

Strings was waiting at the edge of the shelf. She helped pull Harriet up onto it.

"You all right?" asked Harriet.

Strings had wound the chain around the back of

the harp, out of the way. "Yeah. Gonna have some really exciting bruises, that's all. You okay?"

Harriet flexed her aching hands. Her mother wouldn't let her wear fingerless leather gloves because she said they made Harriet look like a biker, not a princess. Harriet thought she might just stash a pair in Mumfrey's saddlebags for times like this.

Then again, if I did that, they'd be in the cage with Mumfrey, so they wouldn't do me any good right now anyway . . .

"I've been slammed into shoes, walls, and piles of rope. I about gagged myself gnawing through a shoelace, and my hands are killing me." She grinned. "So, y'know, all in a day's work."

LET'S DO THIS!

Strings was no coward. She grabbed the shoelace and swung herself down. Her arms rippled with muscles. Harriet was impressed. Apparently playing the harp only *looked* delicate.

The harpster went down hand over hand. Harriet waited until she had reached the floor, then untied the shoelace and slung it over her shoulder. She might need it to get Mumfrey free.

She leaped to the chair back, hopefully for the last time, and climbed down. There was a bad minute when she tried to get a handhold on the chair rungs and her hands did not want to close properly. She dropped to the floor—

—and Strings
caught her.

"Normally that's my job,"
said Harriet.

"Hey, I gotta look out for my drummer," said
Strings. She set Harriet down. "What next?"

"Well, I have to get Mumfrey down."

Mumfrey's cage was on top of the mantelpiece.
The fireplace was made of rough stone. There were
plenty of handholds for a hamster-sized hero.

Mumfrey poked his head over the edge of the mantelpiece. His face lit up when he saw Harriet. "Qwerk!"

"Hush!" hissed Harriet. "Don't wake up the giant!"

She was staring up the fireplace and wondering how she was going to get Mumfrey's cage open at all, when she heard an unexpected voice from the castle door.

"Harriet? Are you in here?"

Strings jumped, startled. Harriet spun around. "Wilbur?!"

CHAPTER 17

It was indeed her best friend, Wilbur. He was leading his riding quail, Hyacinth, and looking around with interest.

"Keep your voice down!" whispered Harriet. "There's an evil giant!"

"Of *course* there is," said Wilbur, but he said it in a whisper.

Harriet introduced hamster and harpster to each other.

"Nice to meet you," said Wilbur.

"I've heard so much about you," said Strings.

"But how did you know I was up here?" said Harriet.

Wilbur flipped his hair out of his face. "So I rode Hyacinth up the beanstalk."

"Cool," said Harriet. "We're rescuing Strings here from an evil giant. We're gonna start a band."

"You know she can't sing, right?" said Wilbur to Strings.

"She's the drummer. She just has to hit stuff."

"Oh, she's very good at that."

Harriet beamed.

"Anyway, now that you're here, Hyacinth can help me get Mumfrey down!"

Hyacinth was craning her neck up to look at Mumfrey in the cage. "Qwerk!" she said, which is Quail for "How dare someone put Mumfrey in a cage!?"

"Qwerk!" replied Mumfrey, which is Quail for "*I know*, right?"

Hyacinth scowled. She was a delicate little riding quail, not a trained battle quail, but nobody put her friends in cages!

FLAP
FLAP
FLAP

She hopped up to the table, took a running leap, and flapped frantically. The movement of stubby quail wings carried her to the top of the mantelpiece.

"Qwerk," she grumbled. "Qwerk, qwerk. Qwer-rrrk—gnff!"

The last bit was as she flipped the latch open and tried to pull the lid back. Mumfrey tried to help by pushing his head up against the underside.

The cage was already hanging partly over the edge. It rocked on the mantel. Wilbur, Strings, and Harriet held their breath.

With much flapping and fluttering and thumping, Hyacinth managed to flip the lid over. "Qwerk!" said Mumfrey happily, which is Quail for "I'm free!"

"Qwerk!" said Hyacinth, which is Quail for "We did it! And my beak is sore!"

Their glee lasted for almost five seconds, and then Mumfrey launched himself out of the cage.

Even in magical kingdoms, the laws of physics still apply most of the time. In this case, the law was a very basic one—that every action has an equal and opposite reaction.

If a battle quail pushes off against the floor of a cage, the quail goes up.

Unfortunately, sometimes it also means that the cage goes down.

The cage teetered on the edge of the mantel—started to lean—and Mumfrey hit the edge with his feet as he tried to bounce free.

It fell.

Harriet watched as the cage fell toward the floor in what seemed like slow motion. She leaped forward, as if a hamster could really stop a cage the size of a small room from falling.

NOOOOOOOOOO...!

The cage struck the floor and shattered into a million pieces.

From the bedroom came the roar of an awakened giant. "Fee fie foe fair! *What is going on in there?*"

CHAPTER 18

Go!" cried Harriet. "Go, go, go! I'll hold him!"

"He's thirty feet tall!" said Strings. "How are you gonna—"

Fortunately Wilbur was there. "Trust Harriet!" he said, helping Strings onto quail-back. "She knows what she's doing at least half the time!"

Harriet tried to work out whether or not that was a compliment. Really, it was more like three-quarters of the time. Maybe even four-fifths. She could hear the giant flinging blankets around as he got up.

She planted herself in front of the bedroom door. She wished she had had time to grab her sword. In her experience, it was a lot easier to make monsters pay attention to you when you had a sword.

Guess I'll just have to improvise . . .

The door slammed back and the giant appeared in the doorway, looking groggy and furious. Harriet could hear the quail scurrying toward the exit.

My job is to make sure he doesn't notice them.

HEY, BUNNY-BUTT!
OVER HERE!

The giant blinked a few times, then looked down.

"Yeah, I'm talking to you!" shouted Harriet. "You're—uh—mean! And smell bad! And your rhyme schemes are terrible!"

"Fee fie foe fart! Nobody insults my art!"

Harriet was briefly struck dumb by the rhyming of *art* and *fart*. Fortunately she did not have to think of a comeback, because the giant tried to step on her.

She dodged out of the way, behind the door, and he had to jerk it open to get at her. That gave her time to dart between the chair legs, where he couldn't stomp.

She shot a glance toward the castle exit. Her friends were nowhere to be seen. Harriet felt like cheering.

Yes! Now I just need to get out myself—

Taking time to look around cost her. The giant snatched her up by the back of her jacket and hauled Harriet into the air in front of his face.

"Um," said Harriet. She had an astonishingly clear view of the giant's nostrils. She hadn't ever given rabbit nostrils much thought. Most rabbits had cute fuzzy noses that sort of folded over.

It turned out that when you were hanging directly in front of a nose bigger than you were, it stopped being cute and fuzzy. The giant's nostrils were the size of storm drains. Harriet could see a wad of snot in one that was the size of Mumfrey's head.

No wonder he snores . . .

"Fee fie foe famster!" roared the giant. "I knew I smelled a mortal hamster!"

"You can't rhyme *hamster* with *famster*," said Harriet. "It's just not right."

"Fee fie foe fimes! As long as it starts with *f* and rhymes!"

Harriet felt that, with this, the time for civilized conversation had passed. She squirmed out of her jacket and jumped.

"Hey!" shouted the giant. He slapped at Harriet. Since she was on his face, this meant that he dealt

himself a stinging blow to the nose while Harriet
half ran, half climbed toward his forehead.

"Stop that!" shouted the giant. "I mean, fee fie
fo—OW!"

The *Ow!* was because Harriet had just kicked him in the eyelid.

He struck at her again, and succeeded in putting his own finger in his eye. "GYAAAAH!"

"That's for *famster!*" shouted Harriet.

All the yelling and thumping had finally succeeded in waking up the goose, who began to honk.

The giant finally got smart. He began shaking his head violently. His ears flapped around him like sails. Harriet had no choice but to cling to the giant's furry forehead. Otherwise she'd be thrown across the room, and the very best-case scenario involved a thirty-foot vertical drop at high speed.

The giant lifted his immense paws and slapped them down over Harriet.

"Fee fie foe fow!" he cried. "I've got you now!"

CHAPTER 19

Harriet had been in tight spots before, but being clenched in a giant's fist was a new one.

She had a sudden appreciation of how Mumfrey must have felt earlier when the giant grabbed him.

"I *knew* it!" said the giant. "I mean, fee fie foe fewit—"

"Oh, don't bother," gasped Harriet.

"Harp is such a liar, saying you left. Harp, you're—"

He turned toward the shelf where Strings had been imprisoned. His eyes swept over the bare boards. *"What?* Where did she go?"

Harriet squirmed. The giant had tightened his grip in surprise and she could feel her ribs creaking.

"Harp!" The giant swept his hand along the shelf, knocking the little pile of bedding apart. He ducked his head to look under it, and saw the missing chain. "She's gone!"

Harriet barely had enough breath, but she laughed anyway.

The giant scowled hugely. He turned and shoved his foot under the goose, who erupted into the air, wings flailing. *"Where is she?"*

"Escaped," gasped Harriet. She managed to wedge her elbow between two fingers and get an inch of space to breathe.

"Tell me where she is," growled the giant, holding her up to eye level. "Tell me, or I'll squeeze until your nasty little hamster eyeballs pop out!"

"If you squeeze me, I'll never tell you!" said Harriet. She hoped that Wilbur had managed to get Strings away, but she knew that she had to buy them as much time as possible.

"Fee fie fo fass!" grumbled the giant. "It appears that we are at an impasse."

Harriet glared. *Impasse* was a really good word and it seemed like the villains always got to use it before she did.

"Let me go and I'll tell you where the harp went," said Harriet.

"Tell me where the harp went, and I'll let you go!" countered the giant.

This extraordinarily tense moment was broken by the goose, who honked once and dropped another egg on the floor.

Both of them looked over at the goose. The goose looked embarrassed and shuffled her feet.

There was no sign of the quail or her friends.

Now I just have to get out of the giant's fist and onto the goose's back. No bird left behind!

I . . . um . . . wish I knew how to do that . . .

Once she was on the goose's back, it should be easy. Admittedly, there wasn't a saddle or reins, but Harriet was determined not to let a little thing like steering stop her. The giant reached down and picked up the cage that had held Mumfrey.

"Sure," she said, "go ahead and put me in that. I'm sure there's no possible way to escape."

"Fee fie fo funny. I bet you think you're funny."

"I know you can't rhyme *funny* with *funny*," said Harriet.

The giant scowled. "Fee fie foe filarious—"

"Hey!" shouted a voice from the doorway. "Hey, giant!"

Once again, it was Wilbur.

CHAPTER 20

The giant wheeled around. Harriet let out a groan, and not just because his fingers had clenched involuntarily.

"My innards!" she muttered. And then: "Wilbur, nooo. . . ."

Harriet couldn't believe this. Usually Wilbur was much better about letting her handle the heroic bits. He was supposed to be getting everybody to safety!

"Fee fie foe fee! Who the heck are you supposed to be?"

Wilbur stood in the doorway. It was so late at night now that it had come around to being early. Harriet could see the light of sunrise outlining her friend's ears.

Wilbur was not an intimidating presence at the best of times, but compared to the giant-sized door frame, he looked practically miniature.

"I'm Wilbur!" he said. "Famed—um—giant-slayer! You better let my friend go!"

The giant stared. So did Harriet.

"You don't look like a giant-slayer," said the giant finally.

He isn't! thought Harriet. *He's a paperboy and sometimes he works in the stables to make extra money! He's gonna get stepped on!*

"I am, though," said Wilbur. "Famous for it. Super-famous." Apparently he did not think this was convincing enough, because after a moment he added, "I've got medals."

"Medals!" said the giant. "For giant-slaying?" Then he seemed to remember himself. "I mean, fee fie foe faying . . ."

The giant looked down at her. "Is he really a giant-slayer?"

Harriet couldn't think of a single person less likely to slay giants than Wilbur, but she certainly wasn't going to say that. "Oh, yes," she said. "Oodles of 'em. At least twenty. Most of them bigger than you, but I imagine he'll make an exception."

"He's a very small giant," said Wilbur, "but of course, they can't all be . . . uh . . ."

". . . Wormeater the Mighty," said Harriet, inventing wildly. "He was huge. Like fifty feet tall."

"No way!" said the giant.

Something odd was going on. Wilbur had come a little way into the castle, but Harriet saw, in the far corner of the door, a hand.

It was waving wildly at . . . someone? And was it holding . . . a potato?

The goose waddled forward, eyes on the potato, and suddenly Harriet realized what was going on. *Of course! The goose eats potatoes! It's Strings luring the goose out!*

If we can convince the giant that Wilbur will slay him, maybe he'll drop me, and that'll be all of us out of the castle—

Unfortunately, the giant did not cooperate.

"No!" he yelled. "I don't believe it! You're too puny to be a giant-slayer! But you might make a good lunch!"

He charged at Wilbur.

The goose, seeing the giant running at her, let out a honk of terror, dropped an egg, and fled through the open door, with Wilbur hot on her webbed heels.

Harriet, for lack of anything better to do, bit the giant on the fingers.

"Ow!" cried the giant.

"Now!" cried Wilbur

"Pull!" cried Strings.

"HONK!" cried the goose.

Chain rattled. The giant shouted. And quite suddenly Harriet was soaring through the air at great speed.

CHAPTER 21

She landed on the clouds and rolled to her feet. Cloud is very springy.

Just outside the doorway, Hyacinth and Strings held either end of the chain that had bound Strings. They had been waiting for the giant to come running. As soon as he had, they had pulled the chain tight, and the giant had tripped over it and gone down hard.

"Brilliant!" said Harriet.

"No time!" said Strings. She yanked the chain

back. She was still tied to Mumfrey. Wilbur leaped onto Hyacinth's back.

The giant was already starting to get up, and he was not happy. "Fee fie—oh, never mind! I'm gonna get you, Harp! And you, giant-slayer!"

Wilbur galloped past Harriet on Hyacinth. Strings went past on Mumfrey.

"Right!" said Harriet. "One left!"

She launched herself at the goose as she waddled by, caught her around the neck, and swung herself up on her back.

The giant climbed to his feet and roared.

"I'll get you!" he shouted. "I'll get you all!"

The goose, honking madly, flapped and waddled across the clouds. As high-speed chases went, she would probably elude the giant for the space of a brief chuckle.

"Fly, you fool!" cried Harriet.

The giant lunged.

The goose suddenly remembered she had wings. She flew.

The wingspan of a great goose is enormous. The giant grabbed for her and only caught a few tail feathers, which made the goose honk in fury. The tips of her wing struck Mumfrey and Strings and sent them rolling.

Harriet, having neither reins nor saddle nor bridle nor any means of actually holding on, threw her arms around the goose's neck and just tried not to fall off.

She darted a glance to one side and saw Mumfrey and Strings righting themselves and shlopping forward. The giant either hadn't seen them or was ignoring them, intent on Harriet and the goose. Wilbur and Hyacinth shlopped past at high speed.

"I'll get you!" shouted the giant. "I'll get you! Fee fie—"

Mumfrey darted in front of him, practically

under his feet. Strings lashed out with the length of chain again and whacked the rabbit smartly across his toes.

He grabbed his foot, hopping on the other one. Birds, hamster, and harp fled.

"Toward the beanstalk!" said Harriet, pointing. "There!"

The quail didn't need to be told twice. They flung themselves across the cloud, toward the distant coil of green.

"Fee fie foe fat! Harp, you're gonna pay for that!" shouted the giant. The cloud rang with his footfalls. In the castle, they would have thundered, but on the soft cloud, they made a squishy thudding noise. It sounded as if they were being chased by a giant sponge.

They reached the beanstalk.

Mumfrey ducked under the goose's wing and paused, looking around for Harriet.

"Go!" shouted Harriet. "Go, go, go!"

The quail hopped down onto the beanstalk.

Strings jangled like a wind chime in a washing machine.

"Right," said Harriet. "Right. Okay. Goose! Err . . . goose?"

The goose stamped her feet, looking nervous.

"Down," said Harriet. "You go down. Climb down, don't fly." The air at the top of the beanstalk was so thin and cold that the goose's wings would be covered in ice.

"Honk?"

DOES THE GOOSE TAKE ORDERS?

. . . SHE'S A *GOOSE.*

"Mumfrey takes orders! He's a bird! Geese are birds!"

"Mumfrey's special!"

Mumfrey rolled his eyes.

Her faithful battle quail started down the beanstalk. His bobbing topknot vanished below the layer of cloud.

The goose seemed to get the idea.

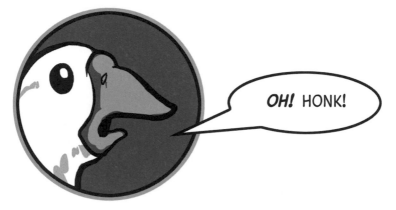

OH! HONK!

She started down, gripping the stalk with her orange feet and her bill. Harriet leaned over and saw powerful hooked claws on the ends of her mount's webbed feet.

Geese are weird, she thought. She'd known a barbarian who insisted on riding a battle goose, but she couldn't imagine trying to keep the thing fed.

They too vanished into the cloud.

Everything was white and wet and freezing. The goose's feathers were adapted to swimming, which meant that they shed water beautifully. Unfortunately, that meant that she was slicker than snail slime and Harriet felt herself sliding off.

She clutched for the feathers, got her grip back, felt a moment of optimism—

And the beanstalk began to shake.

"Fee fie foe feasily! You won't escape that easily!"

The giant was coming down after them.

CHAPTER 22

They broke through the cloud. It was better, because Harriet could see where they were going, but worse because she could see how far away the ground was.

It was really really really really *really* far away.

The beanstalk shuddered rhythmically as the giant climbed, like an old ladder creaking under someone's weight.

"Cut the beanstalk!" screamed Strings.

"With *what?!*" Harriet shouted back.

"I'm surprised you don't have an ax with you," muttered Wilbur. "After you took that class and all . . ."

"People look at you funny if you carry an ax everywhere!"

"Did you tell them you got an A in Brandishing?"

"Well, obviously!"

"Fee fie foe foo!" boomed the giant. "Better look out, I'm coming for you!"

The goose honked in terror. Harriet felt the big feathery body tense underneath her.

She's going to lay an egg. She's terrified, so she's going to lay an egg, and it'll be huge and . . .

Something clicked in Harriet's brain.

She swung herself down from the goose's neck, dangling by a handful of feathers, and grabbed one of the goose's scaly orange ankles.

"Honk!?"

The goose squawked and honked. Harriet swung on the goose's foot and stabbed her sword into the beanstalk for a handhold. "Look—right there! Lay the egg right there!"

There was a spot a few feet down where a leaf had sprouted. The stem formed a ledge where a goose or a quail could stand normally.

"Lay the egg on that ledge!"

"Honk!" said the goose, which is Goose for "I can't do it while you're watching me!"

The beanstalk shook as the giant came into view under the clouds. "I see you!" he roared. "Fee fie foe fun! It won't matter where you run!"

Harriet leaned in and hissed, "If you don't lay that egg, the giant's gonna catch us and he's gonna scramble us like eggs!"

"HONK!"

This was all the incentive the goose needed. She dropped an egg on the ledge and began flapping and flailing downward, shedding feathers. Harriet grabbed for the egg, making sure that it was securely braced against the beanstalk.

"Good goose!"

"Hrroonk!"

Harriet didn't have time to waste. She pulled her sword out of the stem, lifted it up, and slashed downward.

An ocean of egg white poured out of the punctured shell. A yolk twice the size of Harriet oozed after it, and Harriet stabbed the sword into it, popping it open. Orange goo spilled down the beanstalk.

I AM GONNA NEED TO CLEAN THIS THING SO BAD . . .

There was a *lot* of yolk. Harriet had to make her way halfway around the beanstalk to find a spot that wasn't covered in raw egg.

She made her way down, hand over hand. Mumfrey squawked below her, and Harriet yelled back, "Keep moving! I'm coming! I'll be fine!"

"Fee fie foe fot! No, little hamster, you will not!"

Had he seen the egg? It was probably very hard to see over his own enormous feet. Harriet crouched against the beanstalk, her heart pounding.

"I'll eat you feet-first so you can watch it happen!" roared the giant. "I'll keep that harp so weighed down with chains that she won't be able to play 'Twinkle, Twinkle, Little Star'! I'll—"

What exactly he would do was lost as he put his foot squarely into the egg yolk.

It was like grease. His foot went out from under him and he grabbed for the beanstalk, but he was already sliding. His hands went into the yolk next, and suddenly *everything* was slippery.

"Fee fie foe NOOOOOOOO!"

The giant skidded, flailed, and tried to grab hold. His yolk-slicked fingers closed over the beanstalk.

He slipped so far down that he had nearly reached Harriet. One of his feet actually landed below the level of the egg, and for a moment, it looked like he might catch his balance.

Harriet flung herself at his foot, stabbing with her sword.

"Fee fie foe YOWCH!"

The giant jerked his foot back. It was the foot

encased in the shoe with no shoelaces. The toe of the shoe stuck in the beanstalk, and his foot came halfway out.

Harriet jabbed at his heel with her sword.

There was a long teetering moment, and then the shoe came off.

The giant fell.

Unfortunately, so did Harriet.

CHAPTER 23

As Harriet fell, she could see the giant below her, his huge ears streaming behind him. He was flailing wildly and, possibly because of the ears or the wind or the flailing, was rapidly moving off to her left.

This was a comfort. Harriet really didn't want to land on him.

Mumfrey let out a qwerking shriek and dove after her.

Had she been able to, Harriet would have told

him not to bother. Mumfrey was a quail, which are made for flight—short, awkward, flopping flight, but flight nonetheless. He weighed more than Harriet, particularly with Strings still tied to his back, but it was also spread out over a much larger area. His bones were hollow and the feathers caught the air like tiny parachutes.

Harriet, by contrast, came from a line of sturdy little hamsters. Her fur was fluff over solid muscle. She spread herself out to try and present the maximum amount of wind resistance, which didn't help much at all.

Mumfrey fell like a feather. Harriet fell like a rock. There was no way that he was going to catch up to her before she went *squish* on the ground below.

Her only consolation was that her mom wasn't going to get a chance to say "I told you so!"

She instinctively tried to work out the fractions—
if Mumfrey weighs twice as much, but fell two-thirds
as fast, hmm, should probably convert to sixes so we
can cancel out the . . .

Then it occurred to her that this probably wasn't
the best time.

It was a very, very long way to fall, but she
still probably wasn't going to get a chance to be
bored.

Wind howled around her. Her cheek pouches
flapped.

She wasn't particularly afraid of dying. Falling
from a great height had this to recommend it—it
was going to be really, *really* quick.

It was the bit where she wouldn't be *alive* any-
more that bothered her.

She liked living. Living was great. She'd been
looking forward to living for quite a long time yet.

THERE'S SO MANY THINGS I HAVEN'T HIT WITH A SWORD YET! FRACTIONS I HAVEN'T DIVIDED BY! SARCASTIC COMMENTS I HAVEN'T MADE TO WILBUR!

She waited for her life to flash in front of her eyes. She'd lived a very exciting life, and was hoping that there would be some really cool bits.

It did not happen. Harriet was bitterly disappointed. The time she'd shoved a lobster into an Ogrecat's ear would have been *awesome* to see again.

Below her, the giant managed to catch the ends of his huge ears in his hands. They belled out like a parachute.

The giant's descent instantly slowed and Harriet shot past him.

Oh, maaaaan. He's gonna land just fine, and I'm gonna get smooshed! This is the worst day.

Something plucked at her that wasn't the wind.

Harriet twisted around, trying to look over her shoulder. Had Mumfrey somehow caught up to her?

No, the quail was a large speck above her. He was going to have to spread his wings out soon and start gliding, or else he was going to be too close to the ground and might crash. She didn't want him to crash. Just because she'd been dumb and was going to die horribly didn't mean anybody else needed to follow along.

Invisible hands plucked at her again.

"What the heck . . . ?"

The strange unseen hands pressed down on her

feet and pointed her toes. She plummeted toward the earth like a javelin, feet-first, as if she were . . .

Cliff-diving.

OH, COME ON!
NOBODY CLIFF-DIVES FROM
THE STRATOSPHERE!

Nevertheless, she seemed to be doing so.

There was a spell on her that let her cliff-dive safely, but surely it couldn't work if there wasn't water to dive into!

Harriet peered down. The magic hurriedly pushed her head back up, but she had caught a glimpse of the green earth rushing toward her.

Green, not blue. Blue might have been water. She might have had a chance if there was water, but how was she supposed to dive into solid dirt?

She risked another look.

She was actually getting quite near the ground now. She could make out trees as lumpy corrugated green and grass as flat green and there was a road like a giant's shoelace wending through the countryside.

The magic corrected course, tilted her a little, and then—rather strangely, Harriet thought— lifted one of her knees up so that she was leading with a single toe.

"I'm very confused," she informed the wind.

She took one last look, and thought she saw the tiniest flash of light from beneath her, like a glint off metal.

Then the magic grabbed her and pressed her into

a very peculiar shape, foot down, hands at her side.

She saw the trees suddenly grow enormous as she fell past them, and then she struck the ground.

Something around her toe went FWOOOM-*squish* and she felt an absolutely indescribable sensation around her foot, as if she had kicked a block of concrete and someone had pulled it away *at exactly the same speed she was kicking.*

She was standing on the ground.

Harriet looked down.

Her foot hurt. Not because she had just fallen from an unimaginable height, but because it was crammed into the mug that she had left out the morning before.

Impossibly, magically, Harriet Hamsterbone had just executed a perfect cliff-dive from thousands of feet up, into a four-inch deep mug of tea.

CHAPTER 24

There was not a great deal of tea left. Most of it had splashed out and some of it appeared to have boiled off. Also, the mug was now sitting in the middle of a shallow crater that had been blasted into the earth.

Harriet very carefully put her foot down. The ground was hot.

Even magic has to put all that extra energy somewhere.

"Okay," said Harriet. Then she said it again. She

wasn't sure whether she should laugh or cry or do a little dance, so she tried to do all three at once and had to sit down.

Mumfrey thudded to the ground next to her, flapping frantically to slow himself. Strings jangled wildly on his back. A minute later, the goose made a graceless landing and honked frantically.

Strings hastily detached herself from Mumfrey's saddle. The goose ran to her and buried her beak in the harpster's side, making tragic honking noises.

"It's all right," said Strings. "You're fine. No need to keep laying eggs. Please."

"QWERK!" screeched Mumfrey, which is Quail for "You're alive, I thought you were dead, thank the feathery ancestors you're alive, I was so worried—" and flung himself at Harriet, bowling her over.

"Yeah, I'm glad to see you too."

"How are you alive!?" said Strings. "I mean, not that I'm not glad, but *how*?"

"Magic," said Harriet. "I can cliff-dive. It's my only magical skill these days." She extracted herself from under Mumfrey. "Did anyone see what happened to the giant?"

"Well, there was rather a lot of dust from that direction," said Strings, pointing.

Harriet sat up. "Do you think he's . . . um . . ."

"He managed to parachute down on his ears," said Strings. "But you didn't. You should be dead as a doornail."

"Well, they don't call me Harriet the Invincible for nothing," said Harriet.

She started to laugh. She couldn't help it. After a minute, Strings joined in.

"Qwerk," said Mumfrey, which is Quail for "I can't believe you're laughing like an idiot after you nearly *died*."

"Honk," agreed the goose, which is Goose for "Mammals are weird."

"Sure," said Harriet, wiping her eyes. "Sure. Okay."

She sighed. "I suppose we should go deal with the giant . . ."

They re-settled Strings more comfortably on the goose. Harriet climbed back on Mumfrey and took out her sword.

"I'm really *done* with this giant," said Strings. "Like, emotionally. I have moved *past* the giant. I'd like to get on with my life now, in a giant-free fashion."

"Tell me about it," said Harriet, with feeling.

"We still seem to be riding in the direction of the giant, though," said Wilbur.

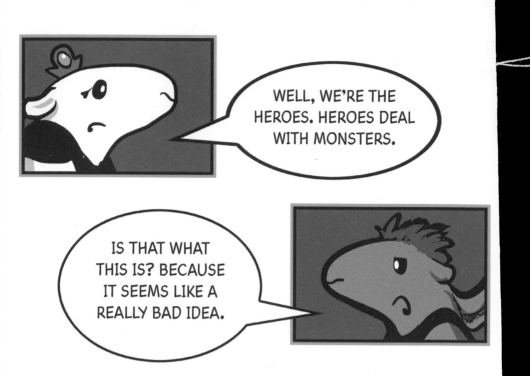

"You and I will be good friends," Wilbur said to Strings. "I tell her that all the time. She doesn't listen to me either."

They reached the clearing where the giant had landed, and saw immediately that there was not going to be a problem.

"Is he . . . dead?" whispered Wilbur.

"No, he's breathing," said Harriet.
The giant lay flat on his back, in obvious pain.

"Fee fie foe fack," he said. "I think I've thrown out my back."

Harriet didn't sheathe her sword, in case the giant was faking. He didn't look like he was faking. He looked like he was afraid to move.

"Uh . . ." said Wilbur. "That happens to our gardener sometimes. His back just stops working and he has to lie down. And you're not supposed to move him."

Harriet eyed the mass of the prone giant skeptically. "I don't think not moving him is gonna be a problem."

"If you're done talking about me, this is reasonably excruciating," said the giant, through gritted teeth.

"If you're expecting sympathy, you're not getting it!" said Harriet. "You squeezed me! You threatened to eat Mumfrey!"

"You kept me chained to a wall for months!" shouted Strings.

"Fine," said the giant. "Look, how about you just get me a heating pad and we'll call it even?"

"Goose, carry me over there so I can kick him," said Strings.

"Honk?"

WHAT DO WE DO?
WE CAN'T JUST LEAVE HIM HERE!
HE'S IN PAIN!

HE'S AN EVIL GIANT, WILBUR!

They stared glumly at the giant.

"I suppose we should contact the local authorities?" said Wilbur.

"I'm a princess," said Harriet. "We're in the hamster kingdom. I kinda *am* the authorities."

"Yeah, but you're more a hitting-things-with-a-sword princess than a rehabilitating-villains princess."

"Being hit with a sword can be very rehabilitating, under the right circumstances."

They sat and looked at the giant some more as he lay groaning.

Harriet was just about to suggest that maybe they make some tea and send a message to her parents' castle when a familiar voice said, "Princess!"

CHAPTER 25

Qwerk . . ." muttered Mumfrey, which is Quail for "Not that guy again!"

The cloaked chipmunk stepped out of the bushes. "Princess! I have an offer that only a fool would—"

He stopped.

He looked from Mumfrey to Harriet and back again. "Oh, bother. I've already tried to sell beans to you, haven't I?"

"You have!" said Harriet indignantly. "And now

there's a ginormous beanstalk sitting over there that somebody's gonna have to clean up! You should *warn* people about those beans!"

OH, YOU GOT THE GROWS-INTO-A-GIANT-BEANSTALK ONE . . . YEAH, THAT ONE'S A PROBLEM.

He waved his remaining two beans in front of Harriet. "But I've got these others! Guaranteed magic! Less likely to pose a threat to air traffic!"

Harriet folded her arms and glared.

". . . I could offer you a discount?" tried the chipmunk.

"What do they do?" asked Harriet.

"Um . . . I *think* this one turns into a ninety-foot-tall pillar of flame and this one grows snow peas, which freeze everything that touches them . . ." He poked the beans in his hand. "Problem is that they aren't labeled, so I don't know which is which."

"Why do you even *have* magic beans like that?" asked Strings.

"Well—"

"Excuse me." Wilbur stepped forward. He jerked a thumb over his shoulder in the direction of the giant. "Do you see that!?"

The chipmunk squinted. "Looks like a giant," he said. "That wasn't one of my beans. None of my beans turn into rabbits."

"He fell off your beanstalk and hurt his back! It's your fault!"

Harriet's mouth dropped open at the enormity of this—well, it wasn't exactly a *lie,* but it was certainly a long way from the whole truth—coming from Wilbur of all people!

HE COULD SUE YOU! YOU SHOULD HAVE PUT WARNING LABELS ON THESE BEANSTALKS!

NOW HOLD ON A MINUTE . . .

"*I'll* give you emotional trauma," muttered Strings, not quite under her breath.

This was a side of Wilbur that Harriet had never seen. She was impressed.

"Look," said the chipmunk a bit desperately, "how was I supposed to know that would happen?"

"It was negligent!" said Wilbur.

"We ought to report you to the fairy godmothers for that! Or the Witch of the Blighted Waste!" added Harriet helpfully.

The chipmunk sighed. "I'll clean it up," he muttered, and vanished sulkily into thin air.

"You'd better!" shouted Harriet, starting to get into the spirit of things. "Or you'll be disbarred and disbanded and disemboweled!"

"Maybe not disemboweled," said Wilbur hurriedly.

"We'll write letters to the editor! We'll put your face on WANTED posters! We'll—"

They looked at the space where the giant had been. It contained a distinct absence of giant.

"You're *really* not supposed to move people with back injuries, though," said Wilbur.

"I don't think teleportation counts," said Harriet. "Where do you think he went?"

"Wherever the chipmunk put him, I guess . . ."

"In his bed," said the chipmunk, re-appearing. "With a heating pad."

"Can you add a copy of *Why We Don't Keep Other People Chained Up in Our House?*" asked Strings.

"Sure," said the chipmunk. He waved his hands. "Anything else you want, while I'm recklessly burning through magical power here? Immortality? Fairy gold? Access to the Supreme Chicken of Enlightenment?"

"I'm good," said Harriet.

"We're cool," said Strings.

"I believe that my client will not pursue legal action," said Wilbur.

"He'd better not," grumbled the chipmunk, and vanished again, this time for good.

CHAPTER 26

"How'd you learn to talk like that, anyway?" asked Harriet.

"Oh." Wilbur looked embarrassed. "Back when I was working for the mouse king. You remember what he was like. There was this guy hanging around the quail stables who was always threatening to sue people. If he stepped in quail poop, he would yell 'I'll sue!' at the quail."

"Did he ever sue anybody?"

"No, he mostly shoveled manure. And I mean,

quail don't even *have* lawyers. That was a weird place to work."

He looked like he didn't really want to talk about it. Harriet recalled that Wilbur had been shoveling quail manure as well, so she decided to change the subject. "It's cool. We'll just start calling you Wilbur the Giant-Slayer now."

PLEASE DON'T. . . .

"So hey, Strings, what will you do now? You're free."

All three were riding along toward Harriet's castle. The beanstalk cast a long shadow behind them. Harriet was not looking forward to having to explain that to her father.

"Well, I still want to form Ironstring," said Strings. "But I'll need to find a few more people. Somebody's gotta play bass."

She glanced over at Harriet. "You still want to be a drummer?"

"Absolutely!"

"Cool. I'll look you up when we're ready to start practicing."

"Just don't plan on a regular tour schedule," said Wilbur. "Harriet attracts adventures like a quail attracts feather-fleas."

Strings shook her head. "And I thought being an enchanted harp was bad . . ."

"Well, I'd hate to get *bored*," said Harriet.

Behind them, there came the quiet
sound of a gigantic beanstalk vanishing
into thin air. (This sounds like
"blorp!" incidentally.)

They rode off toward the castle and, most likely, the next adventure.

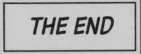

THE END

DON'T MISS THESE OTHER URSULA